www.kindermusik.com

ISBN 1-58987-135-9

Published in 2005 by Kindermusik International, Inc.

Library of Congress Cataloging-in-Publication Data available upon request.

Do-Re-Me & You! is a trademark of Kindermusik International, Inc.

Printed in China
First Printing, December 2005

# Ned Redd
## World
## Traveler
### A Search-and-Find Adventure

by Kelli Kaufmann

...........................

illustrated by Aaron Boyd

# The Mexican Hat Dance

Hi! I'm Ned Redd, World Traveler, and this is my dog Bandana. We're traveling around the world. Do you want to go, too? Come on! The first stop is a city in Mexico. See if you can find me and Bandana and our new friends shown below.

Sleeping Bull

Armadillo Dan

Tumbleweed Diaz

Bella Burro

Juanita Flores

**Explorer:** Look for ten cacti.

**Investigator:** See if you can find the Redd Letter of the Day:

Adios, Mexico!

**Adventurer: Pin the Tail on the Donkey!** Try to memorize where all twelve brown donkeys are in the picture, and then close your eyes and try to put your thumb down on one.

# The Wabash Cannonball

We're riding the rails on the Wabash Cannonball! This train takes us through the American Midwest. Right now we're in Ohio. Look for me and Bandana and all our friends you see below.

Farmer Von Steuben

Bramblefoot Betsy

Phineas J. Scarecrow

Hobo Jo

Conductor McGee

**Explorer:** Look for ten ears of corn.

**Investigator:** See if you can find the Redd Letter of the Day:

So long, Ohio!

Adventurer: Tickets, Please! Help the conductor collect tickets by finding twelve tickets in numerical order.

Good-bye, Kentucky—
Don't be a stranger!

Adventurer: ABC Animals! Starting with anteater and ending with zebra, see if you can find an animal for each letter of the alphabet!

# Give My Regards to Broadway

We are in New York, New York! That's right, we made it to the Big Apple. Look for me and Bandana and these busy New Yorkers.

Statue of Liberteen

Todd the Mime

Intern Billy

Imin Charge

Chloe

Explorer: It's the Big Apple! Look for ten big red apples.

Investigator: See if you can find the Redd Letter of the Day:

Adventurer: Taxi! Try to count all twenty taxis.

# My Wild Irish Rose

Now we're in Ireland! We're hoping to share the luck o' the Irish and find a pot of gold. Help us look and find me, Bandana, and our Irish friends.

Goldie the Leprechaun

Auntie Baa

Dono

Molly O'Kelly

Mr. Blarney Stone

**Explorer:** Look for ten four-leaf clovers.

**Investigator:** See if you can find the Redd Letter of the Day:

R

**Adventurer:** Goldie's Rainbow! Find the right rainbow path between Goldie and his pot of gold. Look for the shortest path that includes all the colors of the rainbow: red, orange, yellow, green, blue, indigo, and violet.

Safe home, Ireland!

# While Stroll Throug

We are in merry old England! Everyone is walking in the park and enjoying the springtime weather. Do you want to join us? Watch out for showers! Look for me and Bandana and these other sights in the park.

May Pole

Candy Rhodes

A Beefeater

Charlotte Mum

Big Ben

Explorer: Look for ten umbrellas.

Investigator: See if you can find the Redd Letter of the Day:

# the Park One Day

Adventurer: Amazing Maze! Try to make your way through the maze in time for tea!

Cheerio, England!

# On the Bridge of Avignon

We're on a bridge in France, and everyone is dancing! Look for me and Bandana and our French friends you see below.

Herb de Provence

Corky

Madam Eiffel

Bridgitte Bow-wow

Hello Sailor

Explorer: Look for ten people wearing black berets.

Investigator: See if you can find the Redd Letter of the Day: U

**Adventurer: Jump and Rhyme!** As you stroll along the bridge, try to find six things in this busy scene that rhyme with "mail" and six things that rhyme with "sea." For a hint, turn to the last page in the book!

*Au revoir, France!*

# Funiculi, Funicula

Now we are in a city in Italy! It's a long walk to the top of the stairs, so look for me and Bandana and these friendly Italians!

Sister Fred

Bill Canto

Mama

Mikey Angelo

Meatball

**Explorer:** Look for ten Italians eating gelato.

**Investigator:** See if you can find the Redd Letter of the Day:

D

**Adventurer: I Step Up!** There are ten objects that start with the letter "I" in this picture. Can you find all ten objects? For a hint, turn to the last page in the book!

**Adventurer:** Upside-Down-Under! See if you can find ten things that are upside down, and two things that aren't but should be.

# Aloha Oe

Aloha from sunny Hawai`i! This is our last stop on an amazing journey. Have a look around this island paradise for me, Bandana, and our Hawaiian friends.

Pamela Plumeria

Queen Lani

Hammond Pineapple

Surfer Doug

Carl Miranda

**Explorer:** Look for ten people wearing leis.

**Investigator:** See if you can find the Redd Letter of the Day:

L

World Traveler,

$\overline{1}\ \overline{2}$   $\overline{1}\ \overline{2}\ \overline{3}\ \overline{4}$   $\overline{5}\ \overline{6}\ \overline{7}\ \overline{3}\ \overline{8}$   $\overline{4}\ \overline{9}\ \overline{2}$   $\overline{1}\ \overline{6}\ \overline{5}\ \overline{10}\ \overline{8}$!

$\overline{1}\ \overline{6}\ \overline{6}$ - $\overline{9}\ \overline{6}\ \overline{6}$!

$\overline{3}\ \overline{2}\ \overline{8}$

Congratulations, World Traveler!

...dventurer: Decode Your Postcard! Use this key to decode Ned's message.

...ey: W/1, E/2, N/3, T/4, R/5, O/6, U/7, D/8, H/9, L/10

# Hints:

**On the Bridge of Avignon:**
Six objects that rhyme with "mail" include pail, nail, sail, whale, snail, and scale. Six objects that rhyme with "sea" include key, tea, ski, bee, pea, and tree. Did you find any more?

**Funiculi, Funicula:**
Ten objects that start with "I" include igloo, iguana, ink bottle, insect, ice skate, island, iris, ivy, ice cube, and iron. Did you find any more?